# Nine Magic Pea-hens

# Nine Magic
# Pea-hens
## and other Serbian Folk Tales

Collected by Vuk Karadžić
Chosen and translated
by John Adlard

Floris Books

First published in English by Floris Books in 1988
© John Adlard, 1988

British Library CIP Data available

ISBN 0–86315–068–3

Printed in Great Britain
by Biddles Ltd, Guildford

This translations is dedicated
to
Pavlo,
a good friend

# Contents

# 1. The girl who got married to a snake

There was once a Queen who had been married for a long time but had never had a child, though she wanted one very much. One evening she prayed and said, "O God, give me a baby, any kind of baby, even a poisonous snake."

Not long after, she had a baby and it was a baby snake. However, the Queen loved him and cared for him as if he had been an ordinary son. The snake didn't speak a single word until he was twenty-two years old, then he said, "Mother, I want to get married."

She replied, "Son, son, what girl would marry a snake? What sort of father would let his daughter be a snake's wife?"

"Please," said the snake again, "find me a wife."

In the end a wife was found. She was a poor girl who would have married anyone to live in a royal palace, but she was a good girl, and beautiful, too, so she and the snake were very happy. After a time she found she was going to have a baby.

"How is it possible," asked the Queen in astonishment, "that you are going to have a baby when you are married to a snake?"

"Every evening," said her daughter-in-law, "when my husband comes to my room, he strips off his snake-skin and underneath he is a young man, the most handsome young man in the whole world. At dawn he puts on the skin once more and becomes a snake again."

When the Queen heard this she was sure that the Prince would be a handsome young man both night and day if only the snake-skin could be destroyed, and the Princess agreed with her. That evening he shed his snake-skin as usual, folded it neatly and slipped it under his pillow. As soon as he was fast asleep his wife very gently drew out the skin and passed it through the window to her mother-in-law, who took it at once to the fire and burned it.

At the very moment the skin burst into flames the Prince woke and cried, "What have you done? Never shall you see me again till in your searching you have worn out a pair of iron shoes and worn down a staff of iron. And the child you are carrying shall never be born until I take you once more in my arms."

Then he vanished.

For three years the Princess waited for the child to be born, and the birth never came. She knew then that she must set off to look for the husband she had lost. She had a pair of iron shoes made, and a staff of iron, and out she went into the world.

After much searching she decided to ask the help of the Mother of the Sun, whom she found stoking up her fire. The Sun's mother wiped her hands on her skirt when she saw the Princess and said, "God preserve you, lovely lady! What are you doing here?"

The Princess told her the story of her marriage and her search. "I want to ask your son," she said, "whether he has seen my husband in his journeys back and forth across the earth."

"Hide yourself for a while behind the door," whispered the Sun's mother. "I hear my son coming home. He will be tired and his face will be clouded with anger, and he may do you harm."

So the Princess hid behind the door. In came the Sun, said good evening to his mother, then cried, "Mother, I smell the scent of a lovely lady!"

His mother answered, "Son, there's no one here. You know that not even the birds can fly so high. How can a lovely lady be in the house?"

The Sun replied, "She is, mother, she is. But let her come out. I'll do her no harm."

So the Princess came out. She told him her sad story, but the Sun had seen no one like her husband and sent her to ask the Moon. The Sun's mother wished her well and gave her a gold distaff and a gold spindle.

Off went the Princess to visit the Moon. She found the Moon's mother in front of her house, kissed her hand and said, "God preserve you, Mother of the Moon!"

"God preserve you, lovely lady! What are you doing here?" replied the Moon's mother.

The Princess told her sad story, then the Moon's mother said, "Hide yourself for a while behind the door. My son is coming home and he will be tired and bad-tempered."

So she hid and the Moon arrived and bade his mother good morning, then said, "Mother, here is the scent of a lovely lady."

She replied, "No, son, there's nobody here. Not even the birds fly so high. How can a lovely lady be in the house?"

The Moon said, "She is, mother, she is. But let her come out. I'll do her no harm."

So the Princess came out. She told him all her troubles, then said, "Bright Moon, you shine all night over the whole earth. Have you seen my husband?"

The Moon replied, "I have not, but go and ask the Wind."

So she went on her way, but before she went the Moon's mother gave her a gold hen with gold chicks.

The Princess came to the Mother of the Wind told her of her sorrows and her hopes. The Wind's mother listened, then said, "Hide yourself, lovely lady, behind the door. My son is coming home angry and boisterous, and he may knock you down."

In came the Wind, puffing and blowing, sending everything flying. He greeted his mother and said, "Mother, here is the scent of a lovely lady."

She replied, "Son, even the birds do not fly so high. How should a lovely lady be here?"

The Wind said, "She is, mother, she is. But let her come out. I'll do her no harm."

The Princess came out and told her story, then the Wind said, "I have seen him. He is in another country. There he is married to another princess and rules as king. My mother shall give you a gold loom with a gold bobbin, and when you come to that kingdom where your husband is, sit down in front of his palace with the gold loom and bobbin, the gold distaff and spindle, and the gold hen and chicks about you."

The Princess did as she was told. When she came to that country her iron shoes and her iron staff crumbled to fine dust. She sat down in front of the palace and the Queen of that country looked through a window and saw her. "Lord, Lord," she said to herself, "I am Queen, but I have no loom or distaff or hen of gold." So she sent a servant to buy these from the Princess.

The Princess replied, "I will sell nothing, but I will give the gold loom to the Queen if she will let me spend one night with her husband."

The Queen agreed, for she wanted the loom very much. The husband did not recognize the Princess in the dark and as soon as his head touched the pillow he fell fast asleep, the Queen having given him a great deal of wine to drink. The Princess cried, "Gracious King, take me in your arms, that our child may be born!" But it was no use. He slept like a log.

The next morning she gave the loom to the Queen and said she would give the distaff, too, for another night with her husband. Again the Queen agreed.

Again the Princess cried, "Gracious King, take me in your arms, that our child may be born!" As before, it was no use. The Queen having given him a good deal of wine to drink, he slept like a log.

Next day the Princess gave the Queen the gold hen in exchange for a third night with her husband. By this time she was in despair. But that same day a guard came to the King and told him that during the night a woman's voice had been calling, "Gracious King, take me in your arms, that our child may be born!"

Hearing this, the King resolved to drink no wine that night and when his first wife came to him he took her in his arms and immediately their child was born. In great joy they returned home, leaving the greedy Queen of that country behind them.

# 2. A castle floating between earth and sky

There was a King who had three sons and a daughter of whom he took great care. One evening, when the girl had grown up, she told her father that she would like to go for a walk with her brothers. The King gave his permission, but as soon as she had stepped outside an enormous dragon swooped down, caught her in his arms and disappeared into the clouds.

Her brothers went back to the palace to tell the King what had happened, then they set out on horseback to try to rescue her.

After a long journey they came to a castle floating between earth and sky. They thought their sister might be in the castle, and wondered how to climb up to it. They decided to cut all the hair from one of the horses, plait it into a rope, attach one end of the rope to an arrow and shoot the arrow into the castle. The two younger brothers thought the eldest brother's horse should be cropped, but he would not agree. The second brother also refused to have his horse cropped, so the youngest had to offer his. When the brothers had made the rope they fired it at the castle where it stuck firmly. The rope was dangling between the castle and the ground, but the eldest and the second brother were afraid to climb up, so the youngest had to go.

Up he went and searched the castle room by room. Soon he found his sister sitting by the dragon who was fast asleep. He drew his sword and struck the dragon with it, but the dragon only stirred in his sleep and murmured, "Something tickled me."

The boy struck again, much harder, but again the dragon only stirred in his sleep and murmured, "Something tickled me."

Then the boy raised his sword high above his head and brought it down on the horrible creature with all the strength he could muster. And this time the dragon rolled over, dead.

The Princess hugged and kissed her brother, then showed him the whole castle. In one room was a black horse with a bridle of pure silver, in the next room was a white horse with a bridle of pure gold, and in a third room a dun horse with a bridle encrusted with precious stones. Beyond these rooms were more rooms. In the first was a girl embroidering with gold thread, in the second a girl spinning with gold thread, and in the third a girl stringing necklaces of pearls.

Having seen all this, the Prince went back to where the dragon lay and heaved its body over the parapet of the castle. It fell to the ground with a tremendous thump, right in front of his brothers. Then his sister clambered down the rope, followed by the three girls, the first with her embroidery, the second with her spinning, the third with her strings of pearls.

Now the two elder brothers were jealous, knowing that when they returned home the youngest would be the hero of this adventure. So they pulled away the rope hanging from the castle before he could come down, found a shepherd-boy who looked like their brother, and rode home with him. They knew their father's eyesight had become so dim that he would think the shepherd was his youngest son. As for the Princess, she was too scared to say anything.

Now from the high castle the youngest Prince could see and hear almost anything that went on in the wide world. Soon he heard that his two brothers and the shepherd-boy were to marry the three girls.

On the day his eldest brother married, he saddled the black horse he had found in the castle, flew on it to the church where the wedding was taking place, knocked the bridegroom down as he was coming out with his bride, then galloped away.

When his second brother married, he saddled the white horse, flew on it to the church where the wedding was taking place, knocked the bridegroom down as he was coming out with his bride, then galloped away.

But when he heard the shepherd-boy was to marry, he saddled the dun horse, flew on it to the church where the wedding was taking place, leapt down and, to the great joy of the whole congregation, claimed the bride as his own.

His father, the King, was astonished to learn what had happened, as well he might. He was very angry with the two elder brothers and decreed that after he had gone his youngest son should become King. And so he did, and a happy reign it proved to be.

# 3. The nightmare

There was once a man who was so troubled by a nightmare that in the end he couldn't get a wink of sleep. He thought that perhaps if he left home the nightmare wouldn't follow him, so he saddled his white mare and galloped off across the world, not caring where he went. But it was no use. Wherever he laid his head, in house or inn, he had scarcely closed his eyes when that terrible nightmare was at him again and he woke up screaming.

One evening he came to a simple inn kept by an old woman. When the old woman had given him his supper and cleared the table and washed the pots and the dishes, she settled down by the lamp to do some sewing.

The poor man told her his story, then he said, "Perhaps I might get a little sleep if I could lie down here and you could watch me while you do your work."

So the old woman went on sewing in the lamplight and her guest lay down and covered himself with a blanket. No sooner had he done this than the old woman heard him cry out and saw him writhing, heaving and struggling. She put down her sewing, took the lamp in her hand and peeped under the blanket. There in the dim light she saw a horrible white, hairy creature pressing down on the sleeping man, biting him, kicking him and strangling him.

The old woman reached for a knife and plunged it deep into that horrible white creature, which at once vanished. Then her guest awoke, fresh and smiling, as if he had had a good night's sleep. He thanked the old woman and thanked God for his deliverance. Then he went out, whistling happily, to saddle his white mare for the journey home.

But his white mare lay on the ground, dead.

# 4. Three rings

There were once two kingdoms: the King of the first had a handsome son, the King of the second a beautiful daughter. The one King had a great desire that his son should marry the other's daughter, so he sent a messenger with a letter.

The other King read the letter very carefully, then he said to the messenger, "Friend, I can give you no answer till I have asked my daughter." The Princess was called and he said, "Daughter, there is a Prince who loves you. Will you marry him?"

"I will not marry him," the Princess replied, "unless he brings me three rings – one from a star, one from the moon and one from the sun itself."

Her father was grieved at this reply. He turned to the messenger and bade him tell his master what the Princess had said, adding that he was sorry there had not been a better answer.

The messenger returned to his King, who was very angry when he heard the Princess's conditions but did not know what to do. He called to the palace all kinds of wise men and women. None of their advice was of the least use. He offered half his kingdom to anyone who could get what the Princess wanted but nobody could help.

The young Prince, broken-hearted, left his father's palace and wandered off by himself.

"There is no one else to ask," he thought in despair. "All the cleverest men in the kingdom have given their opinions and all are of no use." While he was thinking these gloomy thoughts he came upon an old woman sitting on a stone.

"God preserve you," the Prince greeted her.

"God preserve you, too, son," she replied. "You have been happy, you are unhappy, and you will be happy again."

The Prince began to tell her the cause of his unhappiness, but she stopped him.

"Enough, son," she said. "I know who you are and I know your trouble. Now this is what you must do. Take these herbs from my bosom, comb out my coal-black hair and wait with me here till the evening."

The Prince did as he was told. When evening came she said, "Watch the sky, my son, and when the first star appears take out one of the herbs and cry, 'Lord, Lord, send me a ring!' "

Again the Prince did as he was told, and the star leapt in the sky and on to his finger dropped a ring.

"Wait now," said the old woman, "till the moon comes round the mountain, then take out another herb and cry, 'Lord, Lord, send me a ring!' "

The Prince did so, and on to his finger dropped a second ring.

He stayed by the old woman's side as the night wore on, and when daybreak was near she said: "Listen, my son. When you see the sun rise, look at it through my coal-black hair and cry, 'Lord, Lord, send me a ring!' "

The Prince did just as he was told and on to his finger dropped a third ring.

"How can I reward you?" said the Prince, tears of gratitude in his eyes. "You know the King, my father, has offered half his kingdom in return for what you have done."

"I want nothing, son," said the old woman with a sad smile, "But pray for me. Every morning pray for me. I'm an old woman and I've led a sinful life."

The Prince kissed her hand and returned to his father, three rings on his finger, one bearing a star, the second a moon and the third blazing like the sun itself. The two kingdoms rejoiced. And soon after he and the Princess were happily married.

# 5. Tortoise

The Serbs say that before there were tortoises in the world a man baked a flat cake and roasted a fowl, then sat down to eat.

But at that very moment a neighbour knocked at the door and the man quickly put the fowl on the cake and hid them both under a bowl, so that he would not have to share his meal with his neighbour.

When he was alone again and sitting down to eat, he found that, to punish him for his greed, the fowl, flat cake and bowl had been turned into a tortoise.

And that is how tortoises began.

# 6. The girl who was faster than a horse

There was a girl who was not born of a father and a mother. The fairies had fashioned her from snow scooped out of pits where daylight never came, even in the heat of summer. The wind had breathed into her the breath of life and the dew had suckled her. The forest had swaddled her in leaves and the meadow decked her with flowers. She was whiter than snow, redder than roses, brighter than the sun, as no girl was born in this world or ever will be born.

She let it be known far and wide that at such and such a time in such and such a place there would be a race, and if a young man could outstrip her on horseback she would be his. Within a few days this had been proclaimed all over the world and thousands of suitors assembled on the finest horses on earth. Even the Emperor's son came to the racing.

The girl stood on the mark and all the suitors lined up on horseback. She stood among them, with no horse, only her own two legs.

"Over there," she said, "I have placed a golden apple. Whoever reaches it first and picks it up, I will be his, and if I am the first to reach it and pick it up you will all die on the spot, so take care what you are about."

The horsemen looked at each other and every one was sure he would have the girl, and they told one another, "We know for a fact that she won't beat any of us on her own two legs, and God and good luck will help one of us to win her."

And so, when the girl clapped her hands, all dashed forward at once.

The girl soon left them all behind, for small wings sprouted underneath her armpits. At this they all started blaming each other and whipped and spurred their horses and overtook her.

When she saw that, she plucked a single hair from her head and threw it down. At once a fearful forest sprang up and the suitors did not know which way to turn among the trunks. The girl got far ahead again, but the suitors spurred their horses and once more overtook her.

When the girl saw the race was not going well for her, she shed a single tear and, lo and behold, a raging river burst forth from it and almost all the suitors were drowned.

No one now was following the girl but the Emperor's son, and his horse carried him, swimming after her. When he saw that she was leaving him behind again he charged her three times in God's name to stay where she was. She obeyed that solemn injunction and stayed where she was.

Then he snatched her up and set her behind him on the horse, and the horse swam to dry land. The Prince galloped off to the mountains from which he had come, but when he reached the highest mountain peak he looked around, and the girl was nowhere to be seen.

# 7. The nine magic pea-hens

There was once a king who had three sons. In front of his palace was a golden apple tree which each night had a new crop of golden apples.

One morning the King woke up and looked out of his window, as he always did, and saw that the apples had been stolen, every one of them.

Of course he was very annoyed, so that evening he told his eldest son to watch in case the thief came back. The eldest son sat down by the tree, but he wasn't used to staying up all night and fell asleep. It was daylight when he awoke; the birds were singing merrily and all the apples had gone.

The next night the King told his second son to watch. The boy sat down by the tree, but he, too, fell asleep. It was daylight when he awoke; the birds were singing merrily and all the apples had gone.

So the third night the King told his youngest son to watch. This young prince settled down by the tree like his brothers and like them fell asleep. But as the palace clock was striking midnight he woke up again. High above his head on the branches of the magic tree silver blossoms were slowly unfolding. Presently the petals came drifting down and golden apples grew in their place.

Just as the apples ripened a sound was heard in the

sky. Out of the west nine pea-hens came flying. Eight dropped on to the branches of the tree; one landed by the Prince and, the moment she touched earth, turned into a beautiful Princess. She kissed and hugged the Prince, who at once fell in love with her.

At dawn the eight pea-hens that had settled on the tree flew off again and the Princess took her leave of the Prince.

"Leave me one apple," he pleaded.

"I'll leave you two," she said. Then she turned into a bird again and flew away.

The King was very pleased with the apples his son had saved and agreed that he should go on watching. Once again the Prince woke at midnight, saw the tree blossom and the golden apples ripen. Once again the pea-hens came and one turned into a beautiful Princess, who kissed him and hugged him and left him two apples. But the Prince's brothers were envious of his good luck. They found an old woman and paid her to spy on him.

This old woman hid by the tree. When midnight struck she saw it breaking into blossom and the nine pea-hens flying in from the west. Eight dropped on to the branches of the tree and one landed near the Prince and turned into a beautiful Princess. As she kissed and hugged the Prince the old woman took out a long pair of scissors and snipped off one of her golden plaits. At once the Princess turned into a bird again and all nine pea-hens flew away. The Prince seized the old woman and told her she would be punished, but she laughed and vanished, for she was of course a witch.

The Prince didn't suspect that it was his brothers who had paid the old witch to spy on him. He went and told his father what had happened. The pea-hens didn't come back and the Prince made plans to search the whole world for his Princess. The King was very upset. He did all he could to keep the Prince at home, introducing him to all the most beautiful girls in his kingdom, but the Prince wasn't interested.

With just one servant he set out on his quest. He travelled for weeks and weeks, up hill and down dale, till finally he came to a big, dark lake. There was a cottage by this lake and no one lived there but an old woman and her young daughter.

When the Prince saw the old woman he thought for a moment that she might be the old woman who had hidden by the tree, but he decided she couldn't possibly be, so he asked her, "Grandmother, have you seen nine magic pea-hens?"

"Son," said the old woman, "Every day at noon they gather at this lake. But look at my daughter here, a fine figure of a girl and just the wife for a young fellow like you."

The Prince of course had no time for her daughter. All he wanted to know was how long he had to wait before noon. But he accepted a cup of wine from the old woman. Then he took up his position by the lake, on horseback and with his servant beside him.

The old woman had drugged the wine she had given to the Prince and he soon fell asleep in his saddle. As his eyes closed the pea-hens gathered in the sky. Eight landed by the lake and the ninth dropped on to the Prince's horse, turned into a beautiful Princess and began to embrace him, crying, "Wake up, my treasure! Wake up, my sweetheart! Wake up, my only love!"

But he, poor boy, slept like a log. The Princess turned into a bird again and all nine pea-hens flew away.

Just as they vanished into the sky the Prince woke up, rubbed his eyes and said to the servant, "What happened? Have the pea-hens come?"

"The pea-hens have come and gone," said the servant sadly.

Next day the Prince waited again by the big, dark lake. Again he accepted a cup of wine from the old woman and again he fell asleep. The pea-hens came at noon — eight landed by the lake and one dropped on to the Prince's horse, turned into a beautiful Princess and embraced him, saying, "Wake up, my treasure! Wake up, my sweetheart! Wake up, my only love!"

But he, poor boy, slept like a log.

When the Princess saw it was no use she said to the servant, "Tell your master that if he does not see me tomorrow, I shall never be found again in this place." Then she turned into a bird once more and all the pea-hens flew away.

The moment they vanished into the sky the Prince woke up, rubbed his eyes and said to the servant, "Have the pea-hens come?"

"The pea-hens have come and gone," said the servant sadly. "And if you do not see them tomorrow they will never be found again in this place."

You may imagine how nervously the Prince waited on the third day. But again, poor boy, he accepted a cup of wine from the old woman and slept like a log, though the Princess kissed and hugged him, crying, "Wake up, my treasure! Wake up, my sweetheart! Wake up, my only love!"

When she saw it was no use she said to the servant, "Tell your master that if he wants to see me again he must cut off the head of the old woman." Then she turned into a bird once more and flew away.

When the Prince woke up and heard what the Princess had said he was quite mad with grief. He unsheathed his sword and with one stroke cut off the old woman's head. The head, grinning with malice from ear to ear, rolled down a slope and plopped into the lake. The Prince then sent his servant home and set off on foot with a heavy heart, for how was he to know where to find the Princess?

After he had trudged the roads for seven days he found an old man lying by the wayside, too weak to move. The Prince gave him a drink of water, lifted him on to his back and carried him to the next town.

"What can I do to repay your kindness?" asked the old man.

"If only you could tell me where to find nine magic pea-hens!" sighed the Prince.

"Son," said the old man, "God has rewarded your goodness. The palace of the pea-hens stands in the centre of this very town. It is surrounded by an orchard of golden apple trees that shine brightly day and night."

The Prince thanked the old man, made his way through the shining orchard and there, at the door of the palace, saw the Princess waiting to greet him. You can imagine how happy they were that night.

The next morning the Princess turned into a bird once more and set out to fly round the world with the other eight pea-hens. Before she went she kissed the Prince, told him she would be back by nightfall, and gave him a big bunch of keys.

"There," she said, "are the keys of the twelve cellars of this palace. You may look into eleven of them and anything you find there is yours. But the twelfth you must not look into — you must not even open the door."

Soon after the birds had flown away the Prince went down to look at the cellars, and when he came to the twelfth cellar his curiosity was too much for him. He took the key and unlocked the door.

There was nothing in the twelfth cellar but a huge barrel. As the Prince stood looking at it a hoarse voice called from inside, "Brother, brother, give me water! I'm dying of thirst!"

The Prince ran upstairs, fetched a cup of water and poured it into the barrel. But again the voice called, "Brother, brother, give me water! I'm dying of thirst!"

So the Prince ran upstairs once more, fetched a cup of water and poured it in. But again the voice called, "Brother, brother, give me water! I'm dying of thirst!"

So a third time he ran upstairs, fetched a cup of water and poured it in.

Suddenly the great iron hoops of the barrel snapped like paper, the strong timbers shattered into splinters, and the Dragon-King burst out. He flew upstairs and seized the Princess, who was just returning with the other pea-hens. In a moment he had carried her off and all her eight companions fled in terror.

The Prince walked for months looking for the palace of the Dragon-King. Finally he found it. The Dragon was not at home and the Princess was alone. She kissed and hugged him and they lost no time in making their escape.

When the Dragon-King returned he was of course very angry to find the Princess had gone, but he said to his horse, "Shall we go in pursuit of her? Or shall we eat and drink first?"

"Let us eat and drink first," said the horse, "and then we will go in pursuit of her."

So the Dragon-King had his dinner, then got on his horse and chased after the Princess and the Prince, and in a few minutes he had caught up with them, so fast was his horse.

"I could kill you," he said to the Prince. "But I won't, because you gave me three cups of water and saved my life." And he seized the Princess again and carried her off.

The next day the Prince crept up to the palace of the Dragon-King and found that he was out and the Princess all alone. The Princess kissed the Prince and said, "Listen, my love, my treasure. The Dragon told me last night that he got his horse from an old woman who lives on that mountain over there. The horse has a brother who is even faster; he is perhaps the fastest horse in the world. If you could get that other horse from the old woman we could easily escape. Go now, before the Dragon comes home."

The Prince set off with all speed in the direction of the mountain. But as he hurried across the rough country he saw a fish gasping on the ground.

"Brother, brother," cried the fish, "throw me back into the water. And for your kindness take one of my scales, and when you need me rub it and I will help you."

Without further thought the Prince took a scale, placed it in his pocket and threw the fish into the water.

Soon after he heard a cry from behind a rock and found a fox in a trap.

"Brother, brother," pleaded the fox, "free me from this trap. And for your kindness take one of my hairs, and when you need me rub it and I will help you."

At once the Prince freed the fox, took a hair and placed it carefully in his pocket.

Soon after he heard a cry from a bush and found a wolf in a trap.

31

"Brother, brother," howled the wolf, "free me from this trap. And for your kindness take one of my hairs, and when you need me rub it and I will help you."

Immediately the Prince freed the wolf, took a hair and placed it carefully in his pocket. Eventually, he came to the old woman's house, and whistling cheerfully he strode up to the door and knocked.

When the old woman opened the door the Prince thought for a moment that she was the old woman who had hidden by the tree, but he decided she couldn't possibly be, so he said, "Grandmother, I need your fastest horse."

"Son," she replied, "you may have my fastest horse if you will serve three days for him."

"What must I do, grandmother?" the Prince asked.

"Listen, son," she said. "This is my strongest and fastest horse. Take him out into the fields. If you look after him well for three days and three nights I will give him to you. But if you lose him I shall have your head chopped off."

And she laughed.

The Prince led out the horse and sat down on the grass holding the reins. Eventually he fell asleep, and he woke up at midnight to find he was still holding the reins, but the horse had gone. All night he searched and at daybreak he came to a pool. Then he remembered the scale in his pocket and rubbed it.

Immediately the fish popped his head out of the water and said, "Speak, brother!"

"I have lost the old woman's horse," said the Prince.

"The old woman's horse is here with us," came the reply. "He has turned himself into a fish."

The Prince struck the water with the reins and the horse came bounding out.

The next evening he sat on the grass holding the reins and again fell asleep. He woke up at midnight to find he was still holding the reins but the horse had gone. All night he searched and at daybreak came to some rocks. Then he remembered the fox's hair and rubbed it.

Immediately the fox popped up his head from behind a rock and said, "Speak, brother!"

"I have lost the old woman's horse," said the Prince.

"The old woman's horse is here with us," came the reply. "He has turned himself into a fox."

The Prince struck the rocks with the reins and the horse bounded out.

The third evening he sat on the grass holding the reins and again fell asleep. As before he woke up at midnight to find he was still holding the reins but the horse had gone. All night he searched and at daybreak he came to some bushes. And then he remembered the wolf's hair and rubbed it.

Immediately the wolf popped his head out of the bushes and said, "Speak, brother!"

"I have lost the old woman's horse," said the Prince.

"The old woman's horse is here with us," came the reply. "He has turned himself into a wolf."

The Prince struck the bushes with the reins and out bounded the horse. Then he led him back to the old woman, to claim him as his own.

You may imagine how angry the old woman was when she saw them still together.

"Didn't you turn yourself into a fish?" she cried to the horse.

"I did," he replied, "But all the fish are his friends."

"Didn't you turn yourself into a fox?" she bawled.

33

"I did," replied the horse, "But all the foxes are his friends."

"Didn't you turn yourself into a wolf?" she screamed.

"I did," replied the horse, "But all the wolves are his friends."

The old woman was so angry that she started to swell with rage, and then she burst and was never seen again.

As for the Prince, he returned as quickly as he could to the palace of the Dragon-King. Again the Dragon was out, and the Prince lifted the Princess on to his horse and away they went.

When the Dragon came home he was of course very angry to find the Princess had gone and he said to his horse, "Shall we go in pursuit of her? Or shall we eat and drink first?"

The horse replied, "Eat or not, drink or not, you will never catch them now."

Hearing this, the Dragon jumped on his horse and set off in hot pursuit, but try as he would he couldn't catch up with them.

Now the Dragon's horse called to his brother, the horse that was carrying the Prince and Princess, "Brother, brother! Wait for me! Let me catch up with you!"

"Up on your hind legs, off with your rider! Then I'll wait for you," said the other horse.

The Dragon's horse reared up and threw his rider off on to some sharp stones. Then his brother waited for him and the Prince and the Princess now each had a horse to ride. They travelled home to the palace of the King, the Prince's father, in perfect happiness, and eight pea-hens appeared in the sky and circled joyfully overhead.

# 8. Cinders

Some girls were spinning next to a deep pit near a herd of cattle when up came an old man with a white beard right down to his waist.

"Girls," he said, "beware of that pit, for if any of you drop your spindle into it, your mother will at once turn into a cow."

Having said this he vanished, and the girls, wonder-struck, crept close to the rim of the pit and peered down. One of them, the most beautiful girl of all, let her spindle fall in. That evening, when she returned home, there was her mother standing in front of the house, turned into a cow.

The girl drove her mother out to pasture with the other cattle and after some time her father got married again, to a widow with a daughter of her own. From the start this woman hated her stepdaughter because she was much more beautiful than her own child. She would not let her wash, comb her hair or change her clothes, and was always looking for excuses to scold her and ill-treat her.

One morning she gave her a bag full of tow and said, "If you don't spin all this today, don't come home tonight, for I'll kill you if you do." The poor girl drove out the cattle and spun as hard as she could, but when at noon the cattle went to lie in the shade she realized that she had hardly begun the task and she started to cry.

When the cow that had been her mother saw this she asked her what was wrong and the girl told her everything. The cow comforted her and told her not to worry at all.

"I," she said, "will take the tow in my mouth and chew it, and when you see the yarn appear from my ear all you have to do is wind it into a ball."

She was as good as her word. She took the tow in her mouth and chewed it, and the girl took the yarn from her ear and wound it into a ball. The job was finished in no time at all.

In the evening, when the girl brought home the enormous ball, her stepmother was astonished. The next day she gave her an even bigger amount of tow, and when that evening she brought this, too, spun and wound into a ball, the stepmother thought to herself that the girl's friends had been helping her.

So the third day she gave her even more tow and sent her own daughter to spy on her. Lurking nearby, she saw how the cow took the tow and chewed it and how the girl took the yarn and wound it as it came from the cow's ear. She went home and told her mother, who nagged at her husband till he agreed to kill the cow.

When the stepdaughter heard of this she cried and cried. When the cow asked her why she was crying and the girl told her, the cow said, "Hush now, don't cry. Listen."

Then she told her daughter that when they killed her she should not eat her flesh but gather her bones together and bury them under a stone at the back of the house, and when she was in any trouble she should come to the grave and help would be found.

So they killed the cow and ate its flesh, but the girl refused even to taste it, saying she was not hungry and could eat nothing. She gathered all the bones and buried them as the cow had told her. The girl's name was Mara, but from that day on she mostly did the housework — bringing water, preparing meals, washing out barrels, sweeping floors and doing all the other household jobs — and as she was usually by the stove her stepmother and stepsister nicknamed her Cinders.

One Sunday the stepmother, getting ready for church with her daughter, scattered through the house a trough of millet and said to Cinders, "If you don't gather up all this millet and cook dinner by the time we come back from church, I'll kill you."

After they had gone off to church the poor girl stood weeping and said to herself, "I can easily cook dinner, but who will pick up so much millet?" Then she remembered what the cow had said, that when she was in any trouble she should go to the grave and find help.

So off she ran and when she reached the grave what did she see? There stood a great chest, wide open, full of all kinds of precious clothes. On the lid were perched two doves, who said to her, "Mara, take from this chest whichever clothes you fancy, put them on and go to church and we will gather up the millet and do all the other work." Happily she took the first dress she saw, all of silk, put it on and went to church.

At church everyone was astonished at her beauty and her clothes, especially because no one knew who she was or where she came from. No one was more astonished and no one eyed her more than the Emperor's son, who happened to be there.

Just before the end of the service she slipped out of the church, dashed home, pulled off her dress and put it back in the chest, which closed and vanished. Then she ran to the stove and found the millet gathered up, the dinner cooked and everything neat and tidy. Presently, back from church came the step-mother and her daughter, and they couldn't believe their eyes when they saw everything in good order.

The next Sunday the stepmother again got ready for church, with her daughter, and when they were about to set off she scattered even more millet about the house and told Cinders, "If you don't gather up all the millet, cook the dinner and make everything neat and tidy by the time we come back from church, I'll kill you."

After they had left, the girl hurried to her mother's grave and found the chest open as before and on the lid two white doves, who said, "Dress yourself, Mara, and go to church. We will gather the millet and do all the work." From the chest she took a dress of pure silver, put it on and went to church.

The people were even more astonished than before and the Emperor's son couldn't keep his eyes off her.

Just before the end of the service she managed to slip away from the midst of the congregation. She ran home, pulled off the dress, put it back in the chest and went to the stove. When the stepmother and her daughter came back from church they couldn't have been more amazed at the sight of the millet gathered up, the dinner cooked and everything neat and tidy.

On the third Sunday they again prepared for church, and when they were about to go the step-mother scattered even more millet through the house and told her stepdaughter, as before: "If you don't gather up all this millet, cook the dinner and do all the other work by the time we come back from church, I'll kill you."

After they had left, the stepdaughter at once went to her mother's grave and once more found the chest open and two white doves perched on the lid. The doves told her she should dress and go to church and not worry at all about the house. She took out of the chest a dress of pure gold, put it on and went to church.

Everyone was more astonished than ever, and the Emperor's son resolved he would not let her slip away as before, but watch her and see where she went.

Just before the end of the service, as she started to go, he caught hold of her, but she managed to squeeze through the crowd and run off. However, the slipper dropped from her right foot and she had no time to pick it up. The Emperor's son seized it and she escaped with one foot bare. Reaching home, she pulled off her dress, put it back in the chest and went straight to the stove.

The Emperor's son now set out to scour the whole Empire, trying the slipper on the right foot of every girl. But some feet were too long, some too short, some too narrow, some too wide — he couldn't find a foot it fitted. And so, going from house to house, he came one day to Mara's home.

Her stepmother, seeing the Emperor's son coming, hid Mara under a trough in front of the house. When the Emperor's son arrived and asked if there was a girl in the house she told him that there was and brought out her own daughter. The slipper was tried on, but she couldn't even get her toes in.

Then the Emperor's son asked if there was another girl in the house and the stepmother told him there was not. At that the rooster sprang onto the trough and crowed, "Cock-a-doodle-doo! Here she is, under the trough."

Hearing this, the Emperor's son ran to the trough and lifted it up. There beneath it was the girl he had seen in the church. She was dressed in the clothes she had been wearing the last time he had seen her, only she had no slipper on her right foot.

When the Emperor's son caught sight of her he nearly fainted with joy. Then he put the slipper on her right foot and when he saw it not only fitted her but was exactly like that on her left foot he carried her off to his palace and married her.

# 9. The nasty wife

A man was travelling with his wife when they came to a meadow that was freshly mown.

The man said, "Look, wife, how beautiful that new-mown meadow is!"

The wife replied, "There must be something wrong with your eyes if you think it's been mown. It's been clipped."

The man cried out, "God help you, woman. Look, you can see the swathes of hay!"

And so, with the man arguing that it had been mown and his wife arguing that it had been clipped, a brawl began, and the man hit his wife and she started to howl.

She stood by the roadside, close to him, scratched his cheeks with her sharp nails and screamed, "Clipped! Clipped! Clipped!"

As they went on their way again the wife, not looking where she was going, for she was glaring at her husband all the time, stepped into a deep pit, hidden by swathes of hay, and fell to the bottom.

When the man saw that she had tumbled in and couldn't get out, he said, "Well, serve you right!" and continued his journey without even peeping down.

A few days later the man was sorry for what he had done and said to himself, "I'll go and pull her out, if she's still alive. She can't help being what she is, and maybe from now on she'll improve a bit."

Then he took a rope and went back to the pit, let down the rope and called out to her to catch hold of it, so that he could pull her out. When he felt weight on the rope he began to pull, but he was in for a shock – instead of his wife he had fished up the Devil, with his one side white as sheep's wool and the other as black as black could be.

The man was terrified and was going to let go the rope, but the Devil cried, "Hold tight for God's sake! Pull me out of here, then kill me if you don't want to grant me my life; only rescue me from here!" So the man hauled the Devil out of the pit.

The Devil immediately asked the man what good luck had brought him to that pit and what he had been looking for there, and when the man told him that a few days ago his wife had fallen in and that he had come to pull her out, the Devil cried, "For heaven's sake, man! You really liked living with her? You've come to pull her out again? Some time ago I fell into that pit. At first, I admit, life was hard down there, but later I got fairly used to it. But since that confounded woman dropped in on me a few days ago her evil tongue has nearly been the death of me. Try and do without her, please! Leave her where she is and I will grant you anything for having rescued me from her."

Then he plucked a herb from the earth and said, "Take this herb and I will leave you and enter into the Emperor's daughter. From all over the empire doctors and priests and monks will come to cure her and drive me out, but I shall not leave the Princess

42

until you come. You will dress up as a doctor and come and cure her. Only when you burn this herb near her will I leave her. Afterwards the Emperor will give you his daughter and you will be ruler of the empire."

The man took the herb and dropped it into his bag. Then they took their leave and parted. A few days later the news spread that the Emperor's daughter was sick, for the Devil had entered into her. From all over the empire doctors and priests and monks gathered, but in vain. No one could do anything.

Then the man hung the bag with the herb in it round his neck, took a staff in his hand and hurried on foot to the Emperor's capital, and straight to the Emperor's court.

As he approached the room where the Emperor's daughter lay ill he saw a swarm of doctors, priests, monks and bishops praying, anointing her and calling on the Devil to come out of her. But the Devil simply roared at them from inside the girl and jeered at them.

When the man arrived with his bag they would not let him in, so he went directly to the Empress and told her that he, too, was a doctor and that he had a herb which would drive out any number of devils. The Empress, as any mother would, leapt up without wasting a moment and took him to her daughter's room.

As soon as the Devil caught sight of him he called out, "Are you here, brother?"

"I am here," said the man.

"Well, then, do your business and I will come out; but whenever I put in an appearance again you must not come after me, for no good will come of it." (This was said in such a way that no one else could understand what they were talking about).

The man took the herb out of his bag and burned it near the girl, and the Devil left her and she was as sound as the day she was born. All the other doctors, put to shame, made off in different directions, and the Emperor and Empress hugged the man as though he were their own son, then took him to the treasury and changed his clothes and gave him their daughter for wife, and the Emperor gave him half his empire.

Some time passed and the Devil entered the daughter of another Emperor, a neighbour of the first. The whole empire was scoured for a cure and when none was found it was reported that the other Emperor's daughter had been ill, and that the doctor who had cured her was now the Emperor's son-in-law. Then the Emperor wrote to his neighbour and asked him to send the doctor who had cured his daughter so that he might cure his own girl, and he, the Emperor, would give him whatever he demanded. When the other Emperor told his son-in-law, the man remembered what the Devil had said when they parted and replied that he had given up doctoring and no longer knew how to cure.

This reply was sent, but the other Emperor despatched a second letter warning that he would raise an army and declare war if the Emperor did not send him his doctor. When this message reached the Emperor he told his son-in-law there was no help for it, he must go. The son-in-law was aghast, but he made himself ready and went.

When he came to the bedside of the sick princess the Devil was astonished and cried, "Brother, what brings you here? Didn't I tell you not to come after me again?"

"Oh, my brother," said the son-in-law, "I've not come to drive you out of the Emperor's daughter, but to ask you what we are to do. My wife has got out of the pit and wants a word with you because you wouldn't let me rescue her."

"What a disaster! Your wife out of the pit?" cried the Devil. And he sprang out of the Emperor's daughter and into the grey sea and never came back.

# 10. Bekri-Mujo

They say that in Stamboul there was once a Turk called Bekri-Mujo (Bekri means drunkard) who had been left untold riches by his father and spent them all on drink, so that he had no clothes but a coarse blanket, wrapped in which he walked the streets.

One day the Turkish Sultan met him drunk in the street and began to scold him for drinking away such a fortune and being reduced to such a shameful state. But Bekri-Mujo was incorrigible and told the Sultan, "What business is it of yours how much I drink? If I drink it's my own money that pays for it. And if you think I haven't any money, tell me, for how much will you sell me Stamboul?"

The Sultan, though he knew that the man had no money, wondered whether others who had might have been talking to him, and he knew that after he had made a pledge he couldn't withdraw from it, so he replied, "Mujo, I certainly won't sell you the whole of Stamboul, but I'll sell you half of it for (he named a sum), and then we can both, at a pinch, rule together."

To this Mujo replied: "Very well. Tomorrow morning I shall bring you the money." And so they parted.

The next day, when Mujo didn't come with the

money at the appointed time, the Sultan sent for him and Mujo, who was sober now, realized he hadn't the money to buy Stamboul or even half of it. Then the Sultan said he should be killed for telling such a lie and making fun of the Sultan.

Mujo at first begged for forgiveness, but when he saw there was no help he said to the Sultan: "If you mean to, it's easy for you to kill me, but I beg you to do me one favour before you put an end to me. Find in your empire three men – one poor man who has nothing in this world, one blind man who can see nothing, and one cripple with no legs at all. Call them all here and give them fine food and drink, and we two shall watch what they do."

The Sultan agreed and at once ordered three such men to be found and brought to him. Sitting them down side by side he plied them with food and drink, and they feasted well.

When they had eaten and drunk their fill the blind man said, "Thanks be to God and glory to the Sultan, who has given us white bread to eat and red wine to drink!"

At this the cripple, unable to contain himself, cried, "Scoundrel, how do you know the bread is white and the wine red if you can't see? You shall feel my boot in your backside."

The poor man chipped in, "Give him one for me, too. I'll pay you good money for it."

Then Bekri-Mujo said to the Sultan, "You see, glorious Sultan, what drink can do! The blind man has no eyes, the cripple no legs, the poor man no money. But now that they've been drinking the blind man has got eyes, the cripple legs and the poor man money. So it was that I had the money yesterday to buy your Stamboul."

Having seen and heard all this, the Sultan pardoned Bekri-Mujo and granted him his life.

Later the Sultan, wondering at the power wine has and seeing how drunkards pine for it, thought that he might try it just once himself. One evening he ordered the finest wine to be brought and got very drunk. When he woke the next morning he felt ill – his head ached so much that he couldn't lift it from the pillow. As soon as news of this spread through the court all the doctors gathered to tend the Sultan, but the Sultan told them that Bekri-Mujo could cure such an illness better than any doctor and he should be sent for at once.

When Bekri-Mujo came, the Sultan told him how ill he was and why he was ill, then asked him what to do.

Mujo replied, "Drink again what you drank last night and your head will be well again."

The Sultan then asked him, "But what shall I do if, when I am sober once more, my head aches?"

Mujo replied, "Start drinking again."

"And how long will this go on?" asked the Sultan.

"Until," answered Bekri-Mujo, "You are clad in a blanket like me."

# 11. What is whitest?

Two friends from the country were arguing one day over what was the whitest thing to be found in this world. One of them said, "Milk." The other said of course it wasn't milk, so they made a bet.

This done, the man who didn't think milk the whitest thing on earth invited the man who did to supper at his house. After they had eaten and drunk he made up a bed for him, bade him goodnight and went off with the candle. When the guest was asleep his host brought to his bedroom a bowl brim-full of milk, set it on the floor and tiptoed out again.

The guest woke up after an hour or two and, feeling a pressing need, climbed out of bed. In the dark he trod in the milk, slipped, and fell on his face with a tremendous thud. His host came running in, bearing the lighted candle.

"I'm sorry," he said, "but I've won the bet. Light, you see, is whiter than milk."

# 12. The servant who was smarter than his master

A countryman, in hard times, having spent every penny he had, saw there was nothing for it but to enter the service of some rich man. He found a man who was wealthy, but was also a real lout, and he asked if he would take him into his service.

To this the rich man replied, "I will, but what can you do?"

The countryman told him he could cook and bake and so on, and the rich man asked, "How much a year do you want in pay?"

The countryman replied, "Twenty ducats a year, and you must feed and clothe me."

The rich man liked the bargain and received him into his house.

The next day all the other servants, the whole household, got up early to begin their work, but of the new servant there was no sign, so around midday the rich man knocked at his bedroom door. He found the countryman had not yet dressed, but was still in bed.

"Is this how you serve me?" he cried angrily.

"Master," replied the countryman, "I have been waiting for you here since dawn as we agreed."

"What did we agree?" bawled the rich man.

"That you should feed and clothe me," replied the servant. "There are my clothes. I've been waiting for you to come and put them on me."

# 13. Apprentice to the Devil

There was once a man who had only one son. This son said to him one day, "Father, what's to be done? I can't go on like this. I must go out into the world and learn a craft. You see how it is today — anybody who knows the least craft lives much better than any labouring man."

His father argued with him for a long time, telling him that a craft also involved worries and hard work, and that he would be leaving his father all alone. But when he saw it was no use arguing with his son he let him go.

So away he went into the world to find a master. After he had travelled for some time he came to a lake. On the bank of the lake he met a man in green clothes who asked him where he was going.

"I'm going into the world to find a master who will teach me a craft," the boy replied.

The man in the green clothes said, "I am a master. Come with me and learn a craft."

The boy didn't need asking twice. He set off with him but as they were walking beside the lake his new master suddenly jumped into the water and started swimming, calling to the boy, "Come and jump in with me and learn to swim."

The boy began to reply that he couldn't because he was afraid of drowning, but his master answered, "Don't be frightened. Jump."

The boy leapt into the water and started swimming side by side with him. When they came to the middle of the lake the master took the boy by the scruff of the neck and dived with him to the bottom.

It was the Devil! He took the boy to his palace, told an old woman to look after him and teach him, then returned to this world.

When he had gone and the old woman was alone with the boy, she said, "Son, you think that this man is a master such as masters are on earth. He is no such master. He is the Devil. He tricked me, too, and dragged me here, and I am a Christian soul. But listen to what I say. I shall teach you all his craft and whenever he comes he will ask you if you've learned anything, and you must always reply that you've learned nothing at all if you want to get free of him and return to the world."

After a time the Devil came and asked the boy, "What have you learned?"

He replied, "I've learned nothing yet."

And so three years passed, and whenever his master asked him what he had learned the boy replied that he had learned nothing.

Eventually the Devil asked him once more, "Have you learned anything at all?"

The boy answered: "I've learned nothing and I've forgotten what I already knew."

The Devil was furious and said, "If in all this time you've learned nothing you'll never learn anything. Go where your eyes lead you and your legs speed you!"

The boy, who by now had thoroughly mastered the

Devil's craft, at once shot up to the surface of the water, swam to the bank and made off home.

His father, as soon as he saw him, came running out of the house crying, "In God's name, son, where have you been?"

And the son replied, "I have learned a craft."

Some time passed and the day came when a fair was held at a nearby village. Then the son said to the father, "Father, let's go to the fair."

The father replied, "But with what, son, when we've nothing at all?"

"Don't worry about that," answered the son, and they went to the fair.

On their way the son said to the father, "When we are near the fair I shall turn myself into a fine horse, such as will not be found anywhere else in the fair. The whole fair will be astonished by it. And my master will come to buy the horse and whatever you ask for it he will give you. As soon as you have the money don't give him the halter but pull it off my neck and strike it against the ground."

When they got near to the fair the boy changed himself into a horse such as had never been seen. The old man led the horse to the fair and everyone there gathered round and stared at it, nobody daring to ask the price. But then up came the boy's master. He had changed himself into a Turk, winding a turban round his head and letting his clothes down to the ground.

"I want to buy that horse," he said. "Old man, tell me what the price is."

The old man told him, and the Turk paid up without a murmur. As soon as the money was in his hand the old man pulled the halter off the horse's neck and struck it against the ground. In an instant horse and buyer disappeared. The old man, returning with the money, found his son at home.

After a while another fair-day came, and again the son said to his father, "Father, let's go to the fair."

This time the old man didn't say a word, but got up and followed him.

When they got near to the fair the son said to his father: "I shall now change myself into a stall full of merchandise richer and more beautiful than anything else at the fair. Nobody will be able to afford it but my master, who will come and pay you whatever you ask. But don't give him the keys. When you have the money throw them to the ground."

Sure enough, when he turned himself into a stall full of merchandise the whole fair stood admiring it. Up came the son's master, again looking like a Turk. He asked the old man, "How much?" The old man told him, and the Turk paid up. The old man, as soon as the money was in his hand, threw the keys on the ground. In an instant stall and buyer vanished, but instead of the stall there was a dove and instead of the buyer a sparrowhawk chasing the dove.

As they were twisting and turning in the air the Emperor's daughter came out of her father's palace and watched them, and the dove suddenly shot like an arrow towards her hand and became a ring on her finger.

Then the sparrowhawk dropped to the ground, changed himself into a man and went to the Emperor and asked him to take him into his service. He said he would serve for three years and ask for nothing – neither food nor drink nor clothing – only the ring on his daughter's finger. The Emperor received him into his service and promised him what he asked.

So the Devil served the Emperor and the Emperor's

daughter wore the ring, and the ring was very precious to her, because by day it was a ring and by night it was a handsome boy.

The boy told her, "When the time comes for them to take the ring from you, don't give it to anybody but throw it on the ground."

The day came and the Emperor went to his daughter and asked for the ring. She pretended to be angry and threw it on the ground. The ring shattered and became a heap of tiny millet seeds, one of which rolled under the Emperor's boot.

His servant, the Devil, immediately became a sparrow and started to gobble up the seeds. But before he could reach the seed under the Emperor's boot it suddenly turned into a cat and ate the sparrow.

# 14. Hard luck

A gipsy couldn't afford to feed his horse, so he thought he would teach him to fast and he stopped giving him anything to eat. When the horse eventually died of hunger the gipsy said, "What rotten luck! After I've taken all the trouble to teach him to fast, he goes and dies."

## 15. The Devil's bacon

One day a thief spied a side of bacon in a man's loft. That night, when everyone was asleep, he came back to steal it. He unhooked the bacon, hoisted it on to his shoulders and was making his way back along a beam when he lost his footing and fell into the room below where the man was sleeping with his wife and children.

When the thief crashed among them the man leapt to his feet in the dark and cried, "Who's there?"

The thief replied, "I'm the Devil."

Crossing himself the man called out, "What do you want here?"

The thief replied, "Hush, look, I've brought you a side of bacon."

The man was getting more and more frightened and he shouted, "Begone, anathema! And take your bacon with you!"

The thief said, "Well, well, if you don't want it, help me to get it out of here."

The man was only too glad to help get the bacon out of the house if he could get the Devil out too, so the thief went off with the bacon.

# 16.  Saved by a bad wife

Two men were waiting in ambush near a road to kill the man who had murdered their father. When he was in range of their guns and they were on the point of shooting him, they saw that he had another man with him, who said, "Faster, for God's sake! It's getting dark. We'll never reach home tonight."

The murderer replied, "I've nothing to look forward to in getting home. I've a nagging wife and her tongue is worse than a Turkish sword, and anyone who killed me would be doing me a favour."

When the two brothers heard this, the elder said, "Really, when a man has such a bad wife it would be better for us not to kill him but leave him as he is."

And they left without harming a hair of his head.

# 17. A sad story

Near Belgrade, in the village of Nemenikući, there is a church. South-east of the church, on a hillside, there is a stone stuck in the ground, and on the top of the hill two stones side by side. People in those parts say that once two boys fell in love with the same girl and wanted to fight over her in the church in the midst of the congregation, but the girl parted them, saying, "You are both so handsome and honest and so dear to me that I don't know which of you I should choose, and it's not right you should fight over me. I will go and sit on the top of that hill and you shall race up from here. Whoever reaches me first, I will be his, and whoever is left behind must not be angry."

Both agreed. Running up the hill one of them lagged behind and dropped dead from exhaustion. The other, not knowing what had happened to the boy behind him, ran on at full speed up the hill. Arriving at the top of the hill, he fell with his head in the girl's lap and also breathed his last. When the girl saw this, she took a knife from her belt and, stabbing herself, died beside him.

Where they died they buried them so there is one stone on the hillside where the first boy fell and there are two on the summit for the second boy and the girl.

# 18. The bird-girl

A certain king had only one son. When he reached the age for getting married the King told him to go out into the world and find himself a girl. The King's son went off, but he couldn't find himself a girl, though he travelled round the whole world.

When he saw that he couldn't find one, after spending so much time and so much money, he thought of killing himself. He wondered for a while how to do this and then climbed a hill with the idea of throwing himself off it head first.

At the top of the hill he clambered on to a great crag and was just going to fling himself off when he heard a voice telling him, "No, man, no! By the three hundred and sixty-five days of the year!"

He paused and, seeing nobody, asked, "Who are you? Let us see each other, and when you've heard my troubles you won't want to stop me doing away with myself."

A little man appeared, white as a sheep, and told him, "I know what's wrong with you, but listen to me." He pointed with his finger and went on, "You see that hill over there?"

"Yes," said the prince.

"And do you see all that marble on top of it?"

"I do."

"Well then," said the old man. "On the top of that hill there's an old woman with golden hair. Day and night she sits in that place and holds a bird in her lap. Whoever can take that bird from her will be the happiest of men. But beware, you must seize the old woman by the hair, if you can, before she sees you. If she sees you before you catch hold of her hair you will be turned into stone there and then, as were all those young men you see thickly strewn on the hillside like lumps of marble."

Hearing these words the King's son said to himself, "It's all the same to me. I'll go over there and if I manage to seize the old woman by her hair all will go right for me. If not, well, I've already decided to end my life."

Off he went to the other hill. He crept up behind the old woman and, to his joy, she was too busy playing with the bird in the sunshine to notice him, and silently he took hold of her hair.

The old woman let out such a shriek that the hills shook as though there had been an earthquake. But the King's son held on and didn't let her go.

Then the old woman said, "What do you want of me?"

He replied, "I want you to give me that bird in your lap and release all those Christian souls."

She consented and gave him the bird and opened her mouth, and out came a bluish wind which, touching the stone figures, turned them again into living men. The King's son, taking the bird, began to kiss and fondle it, and as he kissed and fondled it, it changed into a most beautiful girl.

When the King's son saw how beautiful she was he fell in love with her and took her home with him. Before they set out the girl gave him a staff telling him it would do whatever he told it to do. The King's son struck a stone with this staff and out poured enough gold for their journey. So they travelled together and came to a great river which they couldn't cross, but he touched the water with his staff and the water rolled back and they crossed. Later they met a pack of wolves, which rushed at them and would have torn them to pieces, but as each wolf attacked, the King's son struck it with his staff, and as he struck each wolf it turned into an anthill.

So, happy and unharmed, the King's son and the bird-girl reached home and got married.

# 19. The Emperor's story

There was once an Emperor who was called Dukljan. One day, as he was hunting among deep clefts and dense bushes he found a lake. He approached it very softly in the hope of coming upon something worth his hunting. As he moved forward toward the lake, he glimpsed a winged horse, and on it a winged man with golden hair reaching down to his heels, emerging from the water.

The Emperor quickly hid himself and peered out to see where this man would go and what he would do. As soon as he was on dry land the man dismounted and took up a kind of flute, long and curving and mottled like a snake, and began to play such music as no ear could bear. All the stones and trees began to sway.

The Emperor was frightened and fired an arrow at him, severely wounding him in both wings. The man fell from his horse.

His screams of pain and despair rang to high heaven, and he cried, "By God, man, you saw me quicker than I saw you!"

The Emperor ran at him with his naked sword, but

the poor creature, wounded as he was, plunged into the lake. The Emperor took the winged horse and mounted it, meaning to gallop home. But scarcely was he in the saddle than wings sprouted from his shoulders, and the Emperor, alarmed, dismounted and led the horse.

After a while the wings disappeared, and so he reached home. There he told his household everything that had happened and put the horse in the stable with the other horses.

Now the Emperor's son, having heard what had happened, went off one morning, without telling his father, and, from his father's description, managed to find the lake. But he didn't move quietly as his father had done. Just before he reached the lake he saw coming out of the water a middle-aged woman with tangled hair, weeping. She fixed him with her eye and he dropped to the ground as if dead.

At the very same moment in the Emperor's stables the winged horse began a mad whinnying and beat with his wings against the stable wall, banging so hard that the whole palace shook. The Emperor leapt up from his chair and went to see what the horse was doing, and the horse said, "If you want to see your son alive again, take me back to the place from which you brought me."

The Emperor was astonished and mounted bareback on the horse, which, as soon as it reached the open fields, flew like lightning towards the lake. There the Emperor found his son lying dead and the woman weeping over him.

The Emperor began wailing for his son, and the horse whinnied to the woman and said, "Now let us exchange son for son, even if the father is a lout."

So the woman breathed upon the Emperor's son

and he came back to life and she gave him back to his father and he gave her the horse.

Nobody is quite sure what this story means. Perhaps some of it has been forgotten. But it is thought that the horse was the woman's son and that the man the Emperor wounded was his father.

# 20. Baldy

There was once an Emperor who had three daughters. The two elder girls married emperors' sons and he decided to leave his empire to the youngest, because she was the most beautiful.

Now the Emperor had a servant who was called Baldy, because he hadn't a hair on his head. Baldy worked all by himself in the garden and that garden was as well looked after as if ten men were working there, and no one could understand it.

The Emperor's daughter often looked out of her window and said to herself, "Goodness, how lovely the garden is and how well it's looked after, and to think that there's only one man working there, a little mouse of a man, too!"

One morning the Emperor's daughter, looking through her window as usual and admiring the garden, noticed Baldy the gardener and called to him, "Goodness, Baldy, how can you keep such a big garden so beautiful?"

He replied, "Young lady, my mistress, if you really want to know, get up a little earlier and you will see."

The next morning, without saying anything to her father and mother, the Emperor's daughter got up very early and stood looking out at the garden. She saw a dragon saddled like a horse come to Baldy and bring him lordly clothes and weapons and also three or four men to work in the garden. Baldy put on the clothes and became quite different – he was no longer a bald man but a fine boy, as fine as fine could be, and he mounted the dragon and cantered about the garden, and from the dragon's nostrils sparks flew. From that day on the Princess lost no opportunity of watching Baldy, but told no one about it.

When many suitors came to ask for her hand in marriage she said that she didn't want to marry anyone but Baldy. The Emperor and Empress, when they heard this, started scolding and swearing at her, but she said, "It's Baldy, or nobody!"

When her father saw there was no help for it he dressed her in poor clothes and had her married to Baldy and gave him a bit of land on the other side of the town. Baldy lived with the Emperor's daughter like any other gardener, earning his bread by taking his vegetables to market. But whenever he wished, he could turn himself into the handsomest of men — he had only to whistle and at once a dragon saddled like a horse appeared bringing him the clothes and weapons of a gentleman.

Some time passed and then all at once enemies attacked the empire from all sides, and the Emperor didn't know which way to turn. He said to himself, "Those daughters I married to emperors' sons are helping me now, but the daughter of whom I hoped the most is married to a clodhopper."

So the Emperor, in his great trouble, sent forth a decree that all who could buckle on a sword should join his armies. The armies marched out, one after the other, against the enemy, and then news came to the Emperor of their defeat. In the end, the Emperor himself rode out with every man that he could find, great and small, including Baldy on an old nag.

Everyone laughed at Baldy, saying, "Now everything will be all right. Baldy's off to battle, he'll make mincemeat of them!"

When the Emperor's men reached the battlefield they set up camp, and Baldy pitched a tent for himself and rested in it for three days.

On the fourth day battle commenced. Baldy whistled and the dragon saddled like a horse appeared before him. He lost no time in donning the fine clothes the dragon had brought, buckled on a sword, sprang into the saddle and joined the fight. As he plunged into the battle the whole enemy army panicked – those who were not cut down by Baldy were trampled by his dragon-horse. And so in a trice the enemy were scattered and ran for their lives.

The Emperor, still in his tent, soon heard the news that there was a hero in his army who had defeated the enemy, and the enemy were now suing for peace. The Emperor immediately ordered this hero to be brought before him, vowing that anything he should ask should be his. But before the messengers could be sent other messengers arrived to tell him the hero was Baldy. The Emperor couldn't believe his ears. "If it was Baldy," he said, "surely he would come to see me?" But a letter came from Baldy which said, "When we return I shall ride home by the Emperor's side."

When peace was made and it was time to go home, Baldy picked up his tent and his bits of luggage, then whistled, and when the dragon came he dressed himself in fine clothes and sprang into the saddle and rode home with the Emperor, who was so full of joy that he wept and decreed that Baldy should be Emperor in his place.

# 21. King and shepherd

There was a King who had a daughter, and she was very beautiful. Her beauty was talked about all over the world. Kings and emperors came to propose marriage or just to look at her and marvel. But her father didn't want her to marry anyone but a man who was cleverer than he was, someone who could fool him in some way.

A rich man in a distant land decided to try and win the King's daughter. He passed through many countries and cities and one day he found himself by the house of another rich man. When he asked if he could spend the night there the master of the house welcomed him and said of course he could. A sheep was killed for the guest, and when it was brought to the dinner-table the master of the house put aside the head for his shepherd who was looking after the flocks on the mountainside.

Next day, at dawn, the traveller went on his way to ask for the hand of the King's daughter. Crossing the mountains he came upon the shepherd of the house where he had spent the night. They talked, and the traveller found that for everything he said the shepherd had a clever reply ready.

The traveller was astonished, and it occurred to him that this boy would be a good suitor for the King's daughter, so he said, "Come over here. I've another little matter to talk to you about."

The shepherd replied, "Wait a bit while I bring in the sheep."

He ran off to round them up, then came back to the traveller and the traveller said, "Listen, I'm off to a kingdom to ask for the hand of the King's daughter. But the King has said that he will give his daughter only to a man who is smarter than he is and can fool him in some way. Now I see that you're a bright fellow and can give good, smart answers, so will you come with me to the King and get the girl for me?"

"I will," the shepherd replied.

So they set off together and came to the city where the King had his court. When they reached the King's gate a sentry stopped them and asked: "Where are you going?"

They replied, "We are going to ask for the hand of the King's daughter."

And the sentry said, "Anyone is free to go and ask for the hand of the King's daughter." So he let them through.

When they were brought before the King the rich man saluted him saying, "God save the King!"

"May God bless you, my sons," the King replied graciously, then, turning to the rich man, he went on, "Why has that rough fellow come with you in his coarse clothes?"

The shepherd gave the rich man no time to reply, but answered the King himself, "I may be a rough fellow in coarse clothes, but I have more wealth than those people in fine clothes, and I have more than three thousand sheep besides. Deep in one valley I milk, in another I make cheese and in a third I carry on the dairy trade."

The King said, "It's good that you should have so much wealth."

But the shepherd replied, "That's not good, it's bad."

So the King asked, "How can it be bad to have so much wealth?"

The shepherd replied, "My milk goes sour, my cheese gets mouldy, I have to throw them away."

"Oh dear," said the King, "that's bad."

The shepherd answered, "That's not bad, that's good."

"How, for heaven's sake?" cried the King.

"I take my oxen and my plough," said the shepherd, "and I plough for three hundred days and sow the whole land with wheat."

The King said, "That's good, that you sowed so much wheat."

The shepherd retorted, "No good at all. Bad."

So the King said, "Why, you poor fellow?"

The shepherd replied, "Instead of wheat, pines and beeches come up."

"Oh, that's bad," said the King.

The shepherd said, "That isn't bad, that's good."

The King cried, "How can it be good when you've lost so much wheat?"

The shepherd explained, "A swarm of bees settle on the pines and beeches, so many that not an inch of their trunks can be seen."

"It's good to have so many bees," said the King.

The shepherd replied, "No good at all. Bad."

"Why, for heaven's sake?" cried the King.

"Because," replied the shepherd, "the July sun comes and melts the honey, which runs all over the valleys."

The King said, "That's really bad."

The shepherd answered, "That's not bad, that's good."

The King cried, "How can it be?"

And the shepherd replied, "I take a flea, kill it, flay it and use its skin to hold three hundred shipments of honey."

Then the King said, "You've been lying!"

The shepherd answered, "If I have lied you have believed me. I've fooled you enough for you to give me your daughter. I've earned her."

The King had no choice but to give the shepherd the girl, and the shepherd gave her to the rich man, who gave the shepherd untold wealth in return.

## 22. I'm not from Sarajevo exactly

A certain Turk, entering a barber's shop to be shaved, was asked where he came from and replied, "From Sarajevo." The barber was a devil for fun and began to praise Sarajevo, saying that all its men were heroes and that they were so tough that they never wet their beards before shaving but used the razor on dry hairs.

The Turk liked this and, making it plain that he was as much a hero as any, asked to be shaved dry. But when the razor had hurt him a good deal and he could stand it no longer, he cried, "Wet me just a little. I'm not from Sarajevo exactly, but from a nearby place."

## 23. The foolish bear

Coming out of his cave in early spring, a bear saw some dogwood in full flower. The other bushes and trees showed no sign of blossom, so he thought that the dogwood's fruit would ripen before anything else. He lay down by it to wait. He continued to lie and wait while all the other fruits ripened in their turn and in their turn withered away.

# 24. The black lamb

An emperor had a son who said to himself that he wouldn't marry until he saw in his dreams a girl who would say to him, "I'll bring you luck and bear you a son with a bright star on his forehead."

He told this to nobody else, but one night in a dream a most beautiful woman appeared to him and said, "Young hero, why don't you get married? There are three poor girls without father or mother living in one house and they sit in three wicker porches, each doing her own work. One embroiders, another knits and the third, singing, sews her trousseau. When you wake, go hunting and ride towards the village nearby. On the way you will meet a black lamb with golden horns, and that lamb will guide you to the house of the three girls."

When the Emperor's son awoke the next morning he was filled with joy and did as the woman had told him. He got up early and, with his servants, went off to hunt. When on his way he met the black lamb he told his servants, "You may go now or you may wait for me here. Expect me when you see me."

He followed the lamb until he sighted the little house with the three porches and in each a girl working as the woman had said. So astonished was he by the beauty of the girls that he couldn't decide which was the loveliest, so he just said, "God save you!"

One of them, the eldest, replied, "May He save you, too!"

The second said, "Good luck to you, fine fellow!" and the third, "Welcome happy, happiest of young men!"

The Emperor's son was astonished by these replies, especially the reply of the youngest sister, and he thought to himself that he really would be the happiest of men if he took her to wife, so he slipped a ring off his own finger and put it on hers, telling her, "You are my betrothed."

Then he left and went home. When he told his father everything that had happened, his father was delighted and ordered celebrations.

Now the older sisters, seeing that the youngest was betrothed before they were, began to think that she would be puffed up with conceit, and they decided to summon a witch, an old woman from the village, and promise her all they possessed if only she would stop the marriage.

This old woman handed them a herb and said, "Give her that to drink in some water tomorrow morning. When she drinks it a maggot will enter her head and she will run off to the mountains. After she reaches the mountains she will never be seen again, for she will be lost in the wilderness and wild beasts will hunt her down. When that young man comes back — he is the Emperor's son — you will tell him that she has run off by herself."

The ruthless pair did as she told them. They gave their sister the herb in some water, and as soon as she had drunk it she began to run this way and that, then she ran off into the wilderness.

The next day the Emperor's son came again to find his betrothed, but her sisters told him that early that morning she had run off, no one knew where, and they pretended to weep and wail before him. As quick as he could the Emperor's son went off into the mountains, riding like a madman.

Suddenly he heard someone calling and weeping, and galloping to where the voice came from, he found his betrothed pinned down by a rock, half dead. He sprang from his horse and ran to her. His eyes filled with tears and he gathered her in his arms and cried, "Oh, my treasure, I'm here!"

She recognized his voice and hugged him and died. When the Emperor's son saw that she was dead he drew a dagger from his belt and killed himself, and the two of them fell together to the ground.

At that very moment – by the grace of God – the very same woman the Emperor's son had seen appeared to his father in his dreams, saying, "Up on your feet! Your son and his betrothed are dead. But take the herb you will find under your pillow and gallop with it to (she named a mountain) where you will find their bodies side by side. Tend your son's wound, squeeze the juice of the herb well into it, anoint the heart of his betrothed and say three times, 'Stand up, unhappy-happy, in the name of God!' "

The Emperor woke in alarm, turned his pillow upside-down and found a herb underneath with a yellow flower. Then he dashed out, sprang into the saddle and took the road to the mountain of which he had been told. There he found his son and bride-to-be lying side by side. He squeezed the juice from the herb into his son's wound and anointed the heart of the girl. He had not finished saying for the third time, "Stand up, unhappy-happy, in the name of

God!'' when they both got to their feet as if nothing had happened.

They were astonished to learn that they had been restored to life. The rejoicing father took them to his palace and had them married, and in the first year the young princess bore a son with a golden star upon his forehead.

# 25. The Jonah

A Turkish landowner in Bosnia, who had in his village a man who was a real Jonah, was getting ready to go on a pilgrimage.

Before he set out he called this Jonah to him and said: "Jonah, I am setting out in God's name on a pilgrimage to Mecca and if you don't prophesy any misfortunes to me on the way I'll give you a load of millet when I return."

"All well and good," replied the Jonah, "but who will reward me if you don't get back?"

# 26. Fairy Mountain

A certain rich man had an only son and after he had brought him up he sent him out into the world, not to seek his fortune but to acquire wisdom and to see, as he travelled the earth, how people have to suffer to live honestly during their short time here. He gave him enough money for the journey and as he was rigging him out he also gave him a bit of good advice, especially warning him to take care of his money. Then he sent him off with his blessing.

As he travelled the world the youth reached a city where he saw a man being taken to the gallows. Astonished at the sight, he ran after the group and asked what crime the poor fellow had committed that he should be put to death. He was told, "This man is heavily in debt and, having nothing to pay to all his creditors, according to the law of this place he must be hanged."

Hearing this, the youth asked the judges, "Sirs, is it possible to purchase this man's life and pay what he owes?"

They replied, "Why not?" And they told him how much the debts amounted to.

So he brought out all the money he had and sold all his clothes, right down to his shirt, and when he had settled the debts the judges delivered the man over to him, and he went off with him across the world begging from door to door.

One evening, as these two were resting side by side, the man saved from the gallows said: "I've had enough of this kind of life, and what makes me even sadder is seeing you suffering these hardships on my account, so let us go to Fairy Mountain. There we shall find my foster-sisters and they will tell me how we can both become rich."

The youth agreed and off they went to Fairy Mountain by strange paths, the man guiding and the youth wearily following. They came at last to a wooded peak whose top touched the moon. The leaves of the trees were of gold and the trunks silver, and in the midst of that mountain was a great flame and smoke from a hearth.

Seeing this, the youth was frightened and asked his companion, "What is it? Some sort of miracle?"

The man replied, "Don't be afraid. Here are my foster-sisters and their mothers. But we two mustn't appear together unexpectedly, so I will go on ahead and let them know that we have arrived and have come to live with them. Wait for me here under this tree. It is made of pure gold and its blossoms are pearls. But take care, don't breathe a word till I come back, for it is a fairy tree. The fairies gather here in summer and if they notice any young man on the mountain, there and then they cast a spell on his eyes and turn him into whatever beast they please."

Having said this, he vanished as if the earth had swallowed him up. The youth stood there for a while, then became bored and began to stroll about the mountainside until he came upon some winged girls dancing in a ring. He hid himself so as to watch them and listen to what they sang. But he was unlucky, for the girl who led the dance noticed him and cast a spell on his eyes and struck him blind and dumb. He was terrified and stood there screaming and weeping until his companion, now with wings on his shoulders, flew to his side, took hold of him and said, "Don't be afraid. What's wrong?"

With his hands the youth indicated that he was blind and dumb. When the man understood he took from his belt a small golden pipe and played until from all sides came fairies, foster-brothers and sisters of that man, countless fairies, bringing medicinal herbs from the mountainside.

They prepared a drink for the youth and anointed his eyes and at once his sight came back and his speech returned, but ten times more beautiful than it was before. Then they received him into their company and gave him a wife, and he acquired great treasures and fine sons and daughters were born to him.

But when he grew old he felt sorry for what he had done and returned home. He found his father on his death-bed and implored his forgiveness, and until his own death he lived a true Christian life.

But as long as he lived he went once every summer to the mountain to visit the fairy company there.

# 27. The Animal Tongue

A certain man had a shepherd who had served him for many years honestly and faithfully. One day, following his sheep, this shepherd heard a hissing in a wood. He didn't know what it was so he plunged into the wood to find out. There he saw a fire and in the midst of the fire a snake hissing. The shepherd stood watching, wondering what the snake would do, for on every side of it flames were leaping and getting closer and closer. Then the snake called from the fire, "Shepherd, for God's sake save me!"

The shepherd held out his staff over the fire and the snake slid along it, then up his arm, and wrapped itself around his neck. This gave the shepherd a shock and he said to the snake, "What's this, devil take it? You're not going to kill the man who saved your life?"

The snake replied, "Have no fear, but carry me home to my father. My father is the King of the Snakes."

Then the shepherd pleaded with him and explained that he couldn't leave his sheep, but the snake told him, "Don't worry. Nothing will happen to the sheep. Only let's go quickly."

The shepherd went with the snake through the woods and finally came to a gate formed of living snakes. As they reached it the snake round the shepherd's neck hissed and these snakes at once disentwined.

Then the snake said to the shepherd, "When we come to my father's court he will give you whatever you ask – silver, gold or precious stones – but don't accept anything, only ask for the Animal Tongue. He'll hum and haw, but in the end he'll give it to you."

With that they came to the court and the snake's father, weeping, asked the snake, "Son, for God's sake, where have you been?" And he heard the whole story of how he had been ringed by fire and rescued by the shepherd.

The King of the Snakes said to the shepherd, "What can I give you for saving my son's life?" The shepherd replied, "There is nothing I want but the Animal Tongue."

"That is not for you," said the King, "for if I gave it to you and you told someone else of it you would at once die, so ask for anything else and I will give it to you."

The shepherd replied, "If you want to give me anything give me the Animal Tongue. If you won't give it to me, then goodbye! There's really nothing else I need." And he started to go.

The King called him back, saying, "Wait! Come over here if you really must have it. Open your mouth."

The shepherd did so and the King of the Snakes spat in his mouth and said, "Now you must spit in my mouth."

The shepherd spat in his mouth and the King spat again in the mouth of the shepherd. This they did three times, then the King of the Snakes told him, "Now you have the Animal Tongue. Farewell, but be

it on your own head if you tell anyone of this gift —
you'll die on the spot!''

The shepherd went back through the woods and as
he went he heard and understood what birds and
plants and everything else in the world were saying to
each other. When he got to his flock and found it
complete and undisturbed, he lay down for a short
rest. Just as he was lying down two ravens flew up
and perched on a tree.

They began to talk in their own tongue, saying, ''If
only that shepherd knew that under the spot where
he lies is a vault full of silver and gold!''

Hearing this, the shepherd went to his master and
told him about it and the master brought a cart and
they dug down to the door of the vault and took the
treasure home.

The master was an honest man and he handed over
all the treasure to his shepherd and said, ''Here, my
son, all this treasure is yours, God has given it to you.
But build yourself a house, marry and live on your
treasure.''

The shepherd took his silver and gold, built himself
a house, got married and little by little came to be
known as the richest man not only in his village but
in all the surrounding countryside. He had his
shepherds and herdsmen for his cattle, his horses and
his pigs.

One Christmas Eve he said to his wife, ''Get ready
wine and plum brandy and everything else we shall
need. Tomorrow we'll go to my grazing grounds and
see that my herdsmen have a merry Christmas.''

His wife did as he told her and made all the prep-
arations. Next day they were at the grazing grounds
and the master said to his herdsmen when the evening
came, ''Now everyone is to sit down together, eat,

drink and be merry, and all this night I will watch the herds myself." So off he went to take care of the beasts.

Around midnight the wolves howled and the dogs barked in reply. The wolves called in their tongue, "May we come and take what we please from the herds? There'll be meat for you, too."

The dogs replied in their tongue, "Come then, if we can eat, too."

But among them there was one old dog who had only two teeth left in his mouth, and he told the wolves, "As long as I have these two teeth in my mouth you shan't harm my master."

All this the master heard and understood. When morning came he ordered all the dogs to be killed, except the old one.

The herdsmen protested, "For God's sake, master, it's a pity!"

But the master only replied, "Do as I said."

Off he went home with his wife, he riding a stallion, she a mare. After a while the wife lagged behind her husband and the stallion whinnied and called back to the mare, "Faster! Faster! What's keeping you?"

The mare replied, "It's easy enough for you. You're carrying one rider and I'm carrying three – my mistress, the child in her womb and the foal in mine."

At this the man turned in his saddle and laughed. His wife heard him, spurred on her horse and drawing alongside him asked him why he had laughed.

"I laughed because I laughed," he retorted.

This didn't satisfy her and she went on pestering her husband to tell her why he laughed.

He stood up to her, saying, "Leave me alone, wife, for God's sake! What's wrong with you? I don't know myself why I laughed."

But the more he stood up to her the more she nagged him to tell her why he laughed.

Eventually the man said, "If I tell you, I shall die on the spot." She, paying no attention to what he had said, went on nagging and made it quite clear he would have to tell her sooner or later. And so they reached home. Dismounting, the man at once ordered a coffin and when it was ready had it put in front of his house, then said to his wife, "Look, now I shall lie in this coffin and tell you why I laughed, but when I tell you I shall die instantly."

So he lay down in the coffin, but took one last look about him and saw that old dog from the herds sitting by him and weeping. As soon as he noticed this he told his wife, "Bring a piece of bread and give it to that dog."

The wife brought the bread and threw it to the dog, but the dog wouldn't even look at it. The cock, however, came up and started pecking it.

"How can you eat, you wretch," cried the dog, "when our master is going to die?"

The cock replied, "Let him die, he's mad. I've a hundred wives. Any one of them would come running to me for a grain of millet and if they're bad-tempered they soon feel the sharpness of my beak. But that fool can't manage one wife."

When the man heard this he sprang up out of the coffin, took a stout stick and called his wife, saying, "Come here wife, I'm going to tell you why!" And he gave her a good thrashing, shouting, "That's why, wife! That's why!"

His wife quietened down and never again did she ask him why he had laughed.

# 28. The three eels

There was once a fisherman who each day, for three days on end, caught nothing in his net but one eel. On the third day, catching the third eel, he was very vexed and said, "The Devil has got into this fishing if I can catch nothing but an eel!"

At this one of the three eels spoke and told him, "Don't go on swearing like that, my poor fellow. You don't know what you've caught. You've caught yourself some great, good luck. One of us three you must kill and chop into four portions. Give one to your wife to eat, the second to your bitch, the third to your mare, and plant the fourth outside your house. Then your wife will bear two sons, your bitch two pups, your mare two foals, and in front of your house will spring up two golden swords."

The fisherman obeyed the eel and did just as he had been told. Within a year everything happened as the eel said it would. His wife bore twins, so did the bitch and the mare, and in front of his house sprang up two golden swords.

When his sons grew up one of them said, "Father, I see that you're a poor man and can't support us, so I'll take one of the horses, one of the dogs and one of the swords and go out into the world. I'm young and I can live by my wits."

Then he turned to his brother and said, "Brother, goodbye. I'm going out into the world. Look after the house, work hard and honour Father, and here is a vial full of water; keep it with you, and when you see that the water is muddy you will know that I am dead." This said, he went on his way.

Travelling across the world he came to a great city, and as he was strolling through it the daughter of the Emperor of that country noticed him and fell hopelessly in love with him. She begged her father to invite him to the palace and he did as she asked. The young man entered the Emperor's palace, and when the girl had had a good look at him and at his sword, dog and horse, nothing in the world seemed to her more handsome and she fell even deeper in love.

So she said to her father, "Father, I want to marry that boy." To this the Emperor agreed and, since the boy had no objection, the matter was soon settled. They were married according to the law.

One evening, standing with this wife by a window, the young man saw not far away a great mountain all blazing with great flames, and he asked her what it was.

She replied, "Don't ask me, my lord! That is a magic mountain that blazes by day and glows by night, and whoever goes to see what it is dies in an instant, for the place is bewitched."

But her husband took no notice of the warning. He mounted his horse, buckled on his sword, whistled to his dog, and off to the mountain he went.

When he reached it he found an old woman sitting on a rock. In one hand she held a staff and in the other a herb of some kind. He asked her what the mountain was and she told him to approach her if he wanted to find out. So he approached her and she took him to a courtyard, walled with the bones of heroes, in which were many people bewitched as though dead. As the young man entered the courtyard he turned into stone, like the others there, and so did his horse and dog.

At that very instant the water in his brother's vial grew muddy and he told his parents that their other son was dead and he would go to look for his body. So he went from place to place, from town to town, till luck brought him to that same city where the Emperor had his palace.

When the Emperor saw him he hurried to his daughter with the good news, crying, "Here's your husband!"

She ran, and seeing a man as like her husband as one half of an apple is to the other, with what seemed the same horse, the same dog, and the same sword, hurried with her father to welcome him, kiss him and lead him into the palace. The Emperor thought it was his son-in-law and the Princess thought it was her husband.

The brother was surprised by this affection, but quickly realized their mistake and began to speak as if he were the girl's husband, the Emperor's son-in-law. When evening came he went to bed with the Princess as if he were her husband, but he pulled out his sword and laid it between them. She was astonished.

Then he got up, stood by the window and asked her, "Wife, tell me, why is that mountain glowing?"

She replied: "For goodness sake! Didn't I tell you on that last evening what sort of mountain it was?"

"What do you mean, what sort?" he asked again.

She replied, "Whoever goes there dies bewitched, and I've been terrified lest you should not get back from there."

Hearing this he was overcome by despair and could hardly wait for dawn. As day broke he buckled on his sword, mounted his horse, whistled to his dog and galloped off to the mountain. When he saw the old woman he drew his sword, sprang from his horse and set his dog on her, without saying a word. The old woman was terrified and begged him not to kill her.

"Bring out my brother!" he cried.

So the old woman brought his brother and restored his life and speech. This done and with the brother quite well again, they took the road home.

On the way the brother who had been bewitched said, "Oh brother, let's go back and free all those who are enchanted, as I was."

This they did. They went back and seized the old woman, took her herb and anointed all the people until they, too, began to move and speak.

When all were fully alive again they killed the old woman, and the two brothers returned to the Emperor's palace while the rest went joyfully to see their families again.

# 29. The Dark Country

They say that a certain Emperor, riding at the head of his army to the end of the world, found himself in the Dark Country, where nothing can ever be seen. Not knowing how to get back, he left a foal behind so that a mare, its mother, would guide him to it out of the blackness.

When they had entered the Dark Country and walked some way into it, they all felt some tiny pebbles under their feet and a voice called through the gloom, "Whoever takes away these stones will be sorry and whoever does not will be sorry too."

Some of the soldiers thought, "If we shall be sorry, why take them?" Others thought, "Let's take one at least."

When they returned from the darkness into the world again, they found that the pebbles were all precious stones. Then those who hadn't brought any out were sorry they hadn't and those who had were sorry they hadn't brought more.

# 30. Ero from the other world

A Turk, with his Turkish wife, was digging his maize-field. At midday he went off to feed and water his horse while his wife stayed to rest in the cool shade. Just then a man called Ero turned up.

"God be with you, lady," he said.

"God be with you, peasant. Where are you from?"

"Lady, I'm from the other world."

"Bless me, are you, and have you seen my Muja there who died a few months ago?"

"How could I not? He's my next-door neighbour."

"How is he then; bless me, what sort of life is he having?"

"Thanks be to God, he is well, but, God help me, he's suffering rather from a shortage of cash to buy tobacco, nor has he anything to pay for coffee when he's with company."

"And will you be going back? Couldn't you take a little money to him from us?"

"Why not? I'm going straight back."

Then the Turkish woman ran over to where her husband had stripped because of the heat and took his purse, and whatever money was in it she gave Ero to carry to Muja. Ero accepted the money, tucked it inside his shirt and made off up the brook.

Just as he disappeared, along came the Turk leading his horse to water and the Turkish woman began, "Oh, my man, wait till you hear what I have to tell you! A peasant was here just now from the other world and he says that our Muja is grieving because he hasn't any cash. He has nothing to buy tobacco with or to pay for coffee when he's in company, so I gave him the money that was in your purse to take to him."

"Which way did he go then?" said the Turk. "Which way did he go?"

And when his wife told him Ero had gone off up the brook, he jumped on the bare back of his horse as fast as he could and rode up the brook in pursuit.

When Ero turned and saw the Turk galloping after him, how he ran! He came to a watermill at the foot of the hill, raced inside and called to the miller, "Run for it, you unlucky mother's son! Here comes a Turk to get you! Now take my cap and I'll take yours, and you run for it over the hill."

The miller, seeing the Turk galloping up the brook, panicked, and there being no time to ask why the Turk should be after him, gave Ero his cap, pulled Ero's on his own head and scampered out of the mill and across the hillside. Ero took the miller's cap, sprinkled a little flour on his clothes, and made himself look like a real miller.

A moment later the Turk arrived, dismounted, and burst in, demanding to know where the man had gone who had just entered the mill.

Ero told him, "There he is, do you see him, running away up the hill."

The Turk said, "Hold my horse."

Ero took the horse and away went the Turk up the hill after the miller, zigzagging through a beechwood.

As soon as he had caught up with him and seized

him he cried, "Where have you put the money you cheated my wife into giving you, to take to Muja in the other world?"

The miller stood crossing himself in astonishment. "God bless you, sir! I haven't seen your wife or Muja or the money."

And so it went on for a whole hour till the Turk realised what had happened and raced headlong back to the watermill.

When he got there, would you believe it, Ero had ridden off on the horse and vanished without trace, and the Turk had to trudge back to his wife.

When his wife noticed he was without the horse she cried, "Where is it, man? What's happened to it?"

The Turk shouted back: "Gone to Muja! You sent him money so that he could buy coffee and tobacco and I've sent him the horse so that he doesn't have to walk everywhere."

# 31.  The girl who was too clever for the Emperor

A poor man lived in a cave and had nothing except a daughter who was very clever and went begging everywhere and taught her father to beg and talk wisely.

One day the poor man came to the Emperor to beg for charity. The Emperor asked him where he was from and who had taught him to talk so wisely. The man told him where he was from and how his daughter had taught him.

"And who did your daughter learn it from?" asked the Emperor.

The poor man replied, "It was God who made her clever, and who gave us our wretched poverty."

Then the Emperor gave him thirty eggs and told him, "Take these to your daughter and tell her that if chicks are hatched from them she shall be well rewarded, and if they aren't I'll have you tortured."

The poor man went back to the cave in tears and told his daughter. She realized that the eggs had been boiled and would never hatch. Then she told her father that he must go and rest and she would take care of everything. He obeyed her and went off to sleep. She took a pot, filled it with water and beans and put it on the fire.

In the morning, when the beans were cooked, she called her father and told him to go off with plough and oxen and plough near the road where the Emperor would pass.

"When you see the Emperor," she said, "take the beans and sow them, calling out, 'Hey, oxen, God grant these boiled beans may sprout!' When the Emperor asks how boiled beans can ever sprout, you reply, 'As chickens hatch from boiled eggs.'"

The poor man obeyed his daughter, went off and started ploughing. When he saw the Emperor coming he started to shout, "Hey, oxen, God grant the boiled beans may sprout!"

Hearing these words, the Emperor stopped on the road and said to the poor man, "How can boiled beans sprout?"

The man replied, "Just as chickens, gracious Emperor, may hatch from boiled eggs."

The Emperor realized at once that it was the poor man's daughter who had taught him that trick. He ordered his servants to seize the man and bring him before him, then he held out a skein of wool, saying, "Take that. From it you have to make ropes and sails and everything necessary for a ship. If you don't you'll lose your head."

In a great fright the poor man took the skein, went off home and told his daughter. His daughter sent him to bed, promising she would deal with everything.

The next day she took a small chunk of wood, then woke her father and said, "Take this wood to the Emperor and tell him to make me a spindle and bobbin and frame and all that's needed, and I'll do everything he commands."

The poor man obeyed his daughter and told the Emperor all she had taught him to say. The Emperor, hearing this, marvelled and stood wondering what to do. Then he took a small cup and said, "Carry this cup to your daughter and tell her to empty the sea and leave it dry land."

The poor man obeyed and, weeping, carried the cup to his daughter and told her all the Emperor had said. The girl bade him leave it till the next day and she would see to everything.

The next day she called her father and gave him a bundle of stalks and said, "Take these to the Emperor and tell him to stop up all the springs and all the lakes with them, then I will empty the sea."

The poor man went off and repeated this to the Emperor, who, seeing the girl was much cleverer than he was, ordered her father to bring her before him. When he had brought her and both had done homage, the Emperor asked, "Guess, girl, what is it that can be heard the farthest?"

The girl replied: "Gracious Emperor, thunder and lies can be heard the farthest."

Then the Emperor grasped his beard, turned to his lords and asked them, "Guess how much my beard is worth."

When some had answered this and others that, the girl told them none of them had guessed correctly, and said, "The Emperor's beard is worth three showers of rain in summer."

The Emperor was amazed and said, "The girl's guess is the best." Then he asked her if she would be his wife and added that it could not be otherwise.

The girl curtseyed and said, "Gracious Emperor, let it be as you will. I ask only that you should sign a promise, that, if ever you are angry with me and turn me out, I may have the right to carry away from your court whatever it is that is dearest to me there."

The Emperor gave his assent and put his hand to it.

After some time had passed the Emperor flew into a rage and told her, "I've had enough of you as a wife. Leave my court and go wherever you can."

The Empress replied, "Gracious Emperor, I will obey. Only let me spend the night here and tomorrow I shall go."

The Emperor consented. Then the Empress, when it was suppertime, mixed brandy with his wine, and certain fragrant herbs, and offered the cup to him saying, "Drink, Emperor, rejoice, for tomorrow we shall part and, believe me, I shall be more joyful than if I stayed with you."

The Emperor drank deep and slept. The Empress had a carriage made ready and took him to the cave that was her new home. When the Emperor woke up in the cave he cried out, "Who brought me here?"

The Empress replied, "I brought you here."

"Why have you done this to me?" asked the Emperor. "Haven't I told you that you are no longer my wife?"

Then, showing the document, she said, "It is true, gracious Emperor, you told me that. But look at this promise you have put your name to, that when I leave your court I may carry away from it whatever is dearest to me there."

Then the Emperor kissed her, and they returned to his court together.

# 32. A problem

A certain Turk left the road to drink from a brook. While he was drinking he was caught by a hajduk — a Serbian guerrilla.

To summon his companion, who had stayed on the road, he called out, "Come over here, I've caught a hajduk!"

His companion shouted back, "If you've caught him, bring him here."

"But he won't come."

"If he won't come," called the other, "let him go."

"I'd let him go, but he won't let me go."

# 33. Peg soup

They say that a soldier came to an old woman's door and asked her for something to eat, and she told him there was nothing to eat in the house.

Then the soldier said, "At least give me a pan and a drop of water, so that I can make peg soup."

The old woman gave him a pan and he put an iron peg in it and poured in water and placed it on the fire.

When the water had warmed up he asked the old woman for a pinch of salt. She gave it to him and he salted the water.

When the water boiled he asked for a little flour. The old woman gave him that, too, just because she was curious to know how the peg soup would turn out, and he dropped it in the water and stirred.

After that he asked for an egg and broke it into the mixture, then for a little dripping, which also went in, and finally he whisked the pan off the fire, took out the peg and devoured his peg soup.

# 34. Once a gipsy, always a gipsy

There was once an emperor with an empress who bore him only girls. One day when she was with child he told her that he would send her packing if she gave birth to another girl.

When the Empress's time came, and again it was a girl, she had a hurried talk with a gipsy in the neighbourhood, who had given birth to a boy the same day, and they exchanged babies.

That done, the Emperor was told the Empress had born him a son. He was overjoyed and there were great celebrations.

But alas for the Empress's secret! When the son grew up and went through the forests hunting with courtiers and servants, he kept on remarking, "What fine wood for making wool cards!" or, "What fine timber for charcoal!"

# 35. The last word

There was a man whose wife always had to have the last word and her poor husband had to give in to her. One day, as they were sitting in front of their house, a great flight of cranes passed by, with one crane flying at the head.

Seeing these cranes, the woman said to her husband, "Look, man, how that crane takes the lead – that's my way, too!"

"It's not, wife," the man said. "He is the leader because all the other cranes must obey him, and you must obey me as your husband, so I am the leader."

"Not you! Me!" replied the wife, and so on and on, "Not you! Me!"

Thus they quarrelled and eventually the woman said to her husband, "Man, if I can't be the leader, I shall die."

"Die then!" retorted the husband. "For once I'll have the last word."

The wife lay down and pretended she had died. She lay like that the whole night and in the morning the husband said, "Get up or I shall call the women to wash you and lay you out."

But she asked, "Am I the leader?" and he replied, "You're not."

Then she said, "If I'm not, they can wash me and lay me out."

Hearing this, the husband went and called the women and they washed her and laid her out.

After this he told her sharply, "Get up or I shall go and announce your death."

"Am I the leader?" she asked him, and when he replied again that she was not, she told him, "If I'm not, go and announce my death."

When the time came for her funeral her husband whispered to her, "Get up! The priest's coming, with the choirboys, to follow you to the grave."

"Am I the leader?" she asked, and when he again replied, "No", she said, "If I'm not, let them follow me to the grave."

Up came the priest and the choirboys, and the people gathered and they carried her out into the courtyard and the clergyman read the last rites and the man, apparently weeping over his wife, hissed to her, "Get up, you wretch! Can't you see that they are going to carry you to the grave?"

"Am I the leader?" she asked. He replied that she was not and she said, "If I'm not, let them carry me to the grave."

So they carried her to the grave and when they had lowered her into it, the priest as usual threw earth upon her.

Then the husband said to everybody, "Go, brothers, softly to my house. I'll be with you in no time at all, only I wish to cover her myself with earth, as I promised her."

So the people left and the husband lowered himself into the grave and called through the lid of the coffin, "Get up, you confounded woman! You're going to be buried under the earth."

"Am I the leader?" she asked once more, and when he replied that she was not, she said, "If I'm not, man, and you're going home, give the people something to eat, and drink to the salvation of my soul and let them bury me."

When the husband saw there was no help for it he lifted the lid and said, "Get up. You're the leader, the Devil take you!"

Then the wife leapt out and ran after the people crying, "Wait, folks! I'm the leader! I'm the leader!"

And the people, when they saw this, thought she had turned into a vampire and they ran! As for the priest, when he heard her cry, "I'm the leader!" he fancied she was thinking of him and he ran as fast as his legs would carry him, while the woman raced helter-skelter after him, crying out, "Wait, priest! I'm the leader!"

When he saw she was gaining ground he fell to the earth, paralysed by fear, and she ran on crying, "I'm the leader!" and so reached home.

# Afterword

The collector of these tales, Vuk Stefanović Karadžić, was born in 1787 at Tršić, a village in Western Serbia, the sixth child of a peasant couple whose first five children had died in infancy. Witches were thought to have killed all five, and Vuk was given his name because it is the Serbian word for wolf and wolves were said to frighten witches.

Since the tragic battle of Kosovo in 1389, when Tsar Lazar and all his nobility had been cut down, Serbia had been part of the Turkish Empire. The Turks lived in the towns, the Serbs in the villages, where they were less exposed to Turkish harassment. There was little education. Vuk, a sickly child, learned reading from a kinsman, Jefto Savić, from a teacher at a school five miles away, and later, as other boys did, from the monks at Tronoša, a monastery not far from Tršić.

In 1804 a successful revolt against the Turks was led by Karadjordje (Black George), the most courageous of the hajduks, men distinguished by their bright blue trousers and the silver discs on their chests. They were part patriotic guerrilla, part brigand, and for long had offered the only effective resistance to Turkish rule. Vuk worked as a clerk to one of Karadjordje's henchmen and returned home to find his father's house burnt to the ground.

In 1805 he crossed the Sava to the Srem province of the Austrian Empire, where many Serbs lived, and went to school at Sremski Karlovci. There he learnt Serbian, German, arithmetic and the catechism.

He was back in Serbia two years later, working as a clerk and continuing his education at a high school. In 1809 ill health forced him to seek relief at sulphur springs in the Banat and at hospitals in Novi Sad and Budapest, where he was given the wooden brace for his left leg and a crutch which he used the rest of his life. The following year, when Jefto Savić was sent as administrator to Brza Palanka in Eastern Serbia, Vuk went with him, and it was while deputising for Savić that he came into contact with the local military commander, Hajduk Veljko, whose portrait, "fierce with black moustachios and a scarlet fez," on a monument in a rose garden at Negotin, was to be admired at the beginning of this century by that formidable traveller, Miss Durham.

The Turks were planning an attack on Serbia. When they invaded Vuk argued that Veljko should take guerrilla action, but the hajduk allowed himself to be besieged in Negotin and was eventually overwhelmed. Soon all Serbia was overrun, but Vuk escaped with many of his compatriots into Austrian territory.

Karadjordje sought asylum in Russia, but Vuk went to Vienna. There he met a Slovene scholar, Jernej Kopitar, censor of Slav books for the Austrian government, with whom he soon established a firm friendship. It was Kopitar who in 1815 mapped out Vuk's life's work for him: a Serbian grammar, a Serbian dictionary, a Serbian New Testament, and collections of folk-songs and folk-tales. Of folk-tales, he told Kopitar, he could produce a little book from the tales he already had in his head. The book appeared in 1821, the stories having previously been printed in the *Srpske Novine*, a Serbian newspaper in Vienna. A larger collection came out in 1853. Some of the stories Vuk had heard at Tršić as a child, some he had heard from Tešan Podrugović, a renowned hajduk, and some came from printed sources or from Serbs settled in the Austrian Empire. The book was dedicated to Jakob Grimm, who greatly admired Vuk and his work.

By this time he had already published his grammar, his

collection of Serbian songs, his dictionary and his translation of the New Testament. The dictionary is more than a dictionary, for it is also a treasury of folk-tales and other folk-material. Defining cuckoo, Vuk writes: "The Serbs say that the cuckoo was once a woman who had a brother who died, and she wept and wailed so much that she turned into a bird. (Some say that her weeping and wailing annoyed the brother so much that he cursed her and so changed her into a bird, and yet others say that God was so irritated by her weeping and wailing that He changed her into a bird). When the cuckoo is heard early in the year in the black woods, people say things will be bad that year for the hajduks. But when the cuckoo cuckoos in the greenwood the hajduks are happy."

In 1818 he married a sensible Viennese girl, Anna, the daughter of his landlady. Their daughter Mina was an attractive, spirited girl and might have married the poet Branko Radičević, who has been called the Serbian Shelley, had he lived long enough. It was Mina who translated her father's folktales into German, Jakob Grimm contributing a preface. Soon after his marriage Vuk had been in Russia, an honoured guest, and four years later he travelled to Germany, where he was received with affection and respect not only by Grimm but also by Goethe, who had shown a lively interest in Serbian culture. Between those two journeys he had spent some time in Serbia, where Prince Miloš Obrenović was gradually winning by sly diplomacy what Karadjordje had failed to win by courage and force of arms. There had been a second, longer stay in Serbia in 1829–32. His aspiration to become Minister of Education and tutor to the Prince (which meant teaching him to read and write) had been thwarted, his work as president of the magistrates' court had been hampered by the corruption of the government and the caprices and cruelty of Miloš, and he had left Serbia as a fugitive threatened with death.

Vuk's reform of the alphabet and his insistence that the language of literature should be the language of the people made him many enemies among Serbian writers and the clergy of the Serbian Orthodox Church. Almost the whole nation divided into Vukists and anti-Vukists, who quarreled violently in the streets and squares, the cafés, the inns and the churches. The young were mostly Vukists. In later years Vuk still travelled widely in the lands where Serbian was spoken, collecting folklore and linguistic material, and wherever he went there were people eager to see him. Mina married, but her husband died not long afterwards and she returned to look after her father. His home had long been a place of pilgrimage for Slavists living in or visiting Vienna, and he welcomed them warmly, though bent with age, a red fez on his head, his grey moustache as long as ever, in a study furnished with a single bookcase, a table and some chairs. On the morning of January 26, 1864, he dictated to his secretary, then went to take a rest and died quietly in his sleep.

While putting his stories into English I have continually remembered a December weekend when, with a Yugoslav girl, I tramped the hills of the Fruška Gora, near the Danube. At nightfall we came to a lonely hostel where there were no other guests but an old woman and her husband. She was a very ordinary-looking old woman, but after we had eaten a simple supper she made us forget our beds for most of the long winter night as she produced story after story, each one perfectly told.

John Adlard

# Pronunciation

c   "ts" as in lo_ts_
ć   a sound between _tu_esday and _ch_alk
č   "ch" as in _ch_alk
dz  "j" as in _J_ohn
j   "y" as in _y_es
š   "sh" as in _sh_eep
ž   as in mea_s_ure

# The Blacksmith and the Fairies
## and other Scottish Folk Tales
### Collected by Elizabeth Howden

A collection of much-loved Scottish folk and fairy-tales sensitively retold with the authority of an experienced story-teller who has heard them from childhood. Written with young children in mind, grown-ups are in danger of enchantment.

# The Wisdom of Fairy Tales

### Rudolf Meyer

The fairy-tale with its archetypal images lives on through changes and decline of civilizations, and is always popular with generations of children.

The prince, the tailor, the miller, Thumbling, Cinderella are images of different elements of our own soul. It is this resonance which endears these figures to us. There is wisdom in these characters deeper than allegory or what can be found in psychoanalysis.

The fairy-tale is a remnant of an old long-forgotten clairvoyance which still lived on here and there. Telling fairy-tales to children today gives spiritual nourishment which later in life can be a source of ideals and imaginative, creative thinking. The author rediscovers the "lost meaning" (as Wilhelm Grimm described it) of these stories.

Floris Books